The Mongrel Within

1

Author: Shayne T Pattie

Editors: Charmaine Hawthorn & Peta-Jane Pattie

Cover Illustrator: Angela Pattie

Preface

Life rarely follows the paths we imagine for ourselves. It bends, breaks, reshapes, and reforms us, sometimes slowly, sometimes in a single catastrophic moment. This is a story about that reshaping. The story of a man born into instability, trained by hardship, saved by connection, and shattered by unimaginable loss.

Steve's journey is not one of clean lines or heroic triumphs. It is a story of survival, of the makeshift armour we build in childhood and carry with us into adulthood, even when it no longer fits. It is a story about identity formed in violence yet tethered to hope; about the scaffolding that love builds; and about what remains when that scaffolding is suddenly taken away.

This book explores the quiet truths that many people carry but seldom speak. Truths that trauma can be both a burden and a teacher; that purpose can be both salvation and obsession; and that grief does not simply wound, it transforms. Steve's life shows us how easily a person can fall into darkness, how quietly depression settles into the corners of a home, and how rage can become both compass and curse. It exemplifies how all behaviours and responses serve a purpose, including the tools we use to survive.

This is not a story about perfection. It is a story about being human. About how we learn, how we cope, how we break, and how we rise. Even if what rises is not what we once were.

This is a work of fiction; a psychological revenge thriller blended with drama and martial-arts-driven crime fiction.

As a psychologist, I wrote this book not simply to tell Steve's story, but to honour the unseen battles many people fight behind closed doors. If you find echoes of your own experiences here, know that you are not alone. There are people and organisations available to assist.

Table of Contents

Environment

Steve grew up in an environment not suitable or designed for children of today. He was trained to see the potential threats around him from birth. Some of his immediate family members were members of a well-known gang that encouraged violence on the streets, among other things.

His other adult family members were either in gaol, from "the wrong side of the street" or were good with blades and other such weapons. When he wasn't the target of violence from adult family members, he witnessed it; watching it as it happened or hearing as it happened on an almost daily basis.

He always had something to eat and had shoes for school. Beyond this, however, he had to find ways to make money or learn to just make do. When he was at home, Steve was okay with hiding his face in books or trying to sleep to escape. He was never sure what to expect when he woke each morning from other adults in his house but assumed this to be the normal. It taught him to be hyper aware of his surroundings watching for any perceived threats. This was reinforced at school.

Steve's school life wasn't much safer than his home life. The kids didn't have weapons, but three on one fights were common, with Steve being quite often singled out as he was one of the smaller children at his school. Yet despite this, Steve still preferred school to home.

In the world Steve grew up in, only the strongest survived, and if you weren't the strongest physically, you had to find other ways to survive. Steve was shorter and slimmer than most of his peers which meant that he was not the strongest; but he was clever, sometimes a little too clever for his own good. Occasionally his intelligence could help him avoid fights, but most of the time his sarcasm got him into trouble. Steve also floated between social groups, never fully fitting into any one group for long. He didn't care that much about fitting in as long as he was able to do what he wanted.

He would use sarcasm like a first language, and this often led to being punched in the face. Getting hit in the face by kids only slightly larger than him was fine because his home environment had taught him to take hits from people much larger than himself, often his parents.

When the school failed to protect Steve, he learned that three on one fights could be won by changing the rules, or more accurately getting rid of the rules that others appeared to be bound by. When larger peers were silly enough to attack Steve by themselves, they were thrown with momentum down flights of stairs, into metal drinking troughs or across classrooms. Steve learned quickly about the many weaknesses of the human body.

One of his peers Francine Annabel Nicolls, was an older female student who targeted Steve. Francine was several grades above Steve and mistook him for an easy target. Perhaps because of her own home life that included violence and mistreatment towards women from men, she was very aggressive in general but unconsciously chose Steve as her target. She would often taunt him and externalise her own pain towards Steve.

One day Steve had enough and walked towards Francine. Francine then swung a punch at Steve and without thought, he used her momentum and sent her face first into a metal drinking trough. Steve then walked away feeling the situation was finished. He did not know that Francine had vowed in that moment to make Steve pay and feel the same hurt.

The combination of Francine's own struggles combined with feelings of powerlessness and helplessness she felt from a smaller and younger person throwing her, would fuel her anger for many years; until the day Steve would experience the outcome of this anger.

Steve's environment taught him how to play dirty, how to take hits, how to use his brain and wits, and most importantly how to survive. Even in play, when his peers allowed him to be part of games, games that involved sword fighting with rulers or knuckle flinch competitions, he naturally would target the weaknesses and think about victory and not fun like some of his peers. For him victory was the fun, it was the ultimate point; why else would anyone want to play these types of games?

He would almost always win the sword fighting with rulers as he would aim for the opponents' knuckles and not the ruler. He would also almost always win the knuckle flinch competitions as he would target the soft muscle between the hand knuckles. Always chasing the victory.

Instability and violence shaped his world; it was his normal. Where some failed to thrive in this environment, Steve became more adaptable. He absorbed the negative and began to form a way of living that would later become a key strength and a key weakness in his identity and character.

There were minor benefits to his intelligence as a child with some teachers having a soft spot for Steve. These teachers would often encourage his learning. This was helpful for Steve and gave him something other than survival and violence to focus on. In these brief moments in the classroom, these teachers helped grow a part of Steve that he did not fully understand.

These brief moments helped build something that was healthy and fun but not required for survival. This platform had been slightly built by his parents, but the teachers' methods and the classroom environment were much less stressful than the home learning environment which helped fuel and support his intelligence. For these brief moments in class, Steve felt what other people later told him to be a type of love.

Martial Arts

It wasn't until his teenage years that Steve was accidentally exposed to formal martial arts training. His hyperawareness and his curiosity led to potentially one of the best coping tools available to him.

During one lunch break Steve walked past a classroom that had people doing what looked to be a sport. This was initially confusing for Steve, because the room they were using was known as the "Drama room" and was not advertised as anything else. On closer inspection, Steve discovered that one of his teachers was teaching a type of martial art and that some of his peers were involved.

When he opened the door, he noticed that the instructor was wearing a white uniform (known as a Gi) and that the martial art involved sparring. Steve was curious and at first just watched. Then the following day he returned and decided to give it a go. When he eventually joined, and after several weeks of training during school lunch times, he learned that this martial art not only involved sparring, but also distance drills, patterns and group patterns.

Initially, training felt unusual but positive. Unusual, not because people were punching, kicking and blocking, but because they were doing this without external expressions of anger. Until this point in Steve's life, violence was an answer to a problem many people in his environment seemed to have or seek. Due to his early childhood and natural focus on victory, Steve quickly excelled. His dirty fighting was becoming retrained; his pure aggression was being redirected, redirected into something positive. It also offered stability.

Steve began to learn the difference between fighting and survival. His sarcasm was also still there, but a level of humour also began to emerge, alongside his improvement in self-confidence.

He graded quickly in the martial art and was financially supported by his teachers when his family couldn't. His teacher saw something in him that his early childhood teacher had and encouraged his training as a result.

When Steve entered his first tournament, he might have felt nervous, but he had learned enough self-reliance that he assumed he would win, which he did. Steve won many tournaments in single and group competitions. In the fighting tournaments he found ways to win that were within the rules but were not necessarily morally right. He would dig his punches in deeper when punching towards the mid-section and he would kick toward the weakest points in his opponent.

In the pattern competition his ability to focus and channel his anger improved his expression of the patterns leading to many victories. He found two similarly minded people and the three of them were able to enter and win all group pattern competitions. All these martial arts experiences were teaching Steve the utility of aggression without anger, and how to use it as a last resort, not the first as his home environment had demonstrated.

However, as Steve had already learned many times over, life wasn't smooth sailing. Just as his identity seemed to be forming into a more positive expression of self and just as his training was about to be taken to the next level with an upcoming grading, his environment forcibly changed. Steve was given several weeks to say his goodbyes. Say goodbye to the recent people who had been positive supports, and to say goodbye to the only life he had known.

Martial arts training was teaching him control. The same control that he would soon lose, regain, lose again, and then finally regain and manipulate into something more.

Forced Change

His family was moving and there was nothing that Steve could say or do to stop this from happening. He would miss the positive martial arts environment but would also oddly miss the other aspects. Whilst these other aspects had included a lot of violence from his parents and peers, it was all he had known. He did not want to leave as the little stability he had known felt comfortable, even if it wasn't the safest. But he had no choice.

There was the illusion of choice that was initially provided by his parents about staying a little longer in less-than-ideal housing conditions or moving to a new location with family. Steve chose the first option, but this was ignored and he was forced to go with the second.

He didn't cry about the move, at least not openly. He had learned from a very young age that crying meant more punishment, it meant more ridicule, there was no learned positive that ever came from crying.

When he arrived in the new environment, he quickly appreciated his last school. This new school had many more peers, and no martial arts. Steve would have to start again, but he was adaptable, so adapt he would do.

He searched for something in the new environment to fill the hole. Eventually he found this new something, in another form of martial art. Again, Steve began to excel. This new martial art didn't have much fighting but had lots of patterns and sparring drills. His instructors appeared to see the same thing previous teachers and instructors had seen and he was supported to succeed. He learned new ways of attacking and defending including some interesting ways to close and open distance. Things were looking up as Steve excelled halfway to his blackbelt within six months. Before this too was taken from him against his will.

His parents stopped Steve training in martial arts not understanding what it represented and there was nothing that Steve could do about this. Despite this, there was still a hole to be filled. This reinforced to Steve that attachment to any one thing, and the outward appreciation of this, was a negative and left you vulnerable to non-physical attack from others. The type of attacks that could not be punched or kicked, could not be defended in the traditional manner, and the type that Steve was still struggling to understand. However, he did learn that nothing is guaranteed and that everything can be taken. A lesson he would later learn again, in a big way.

Steve's unconscious search to fill the hole and the lack of support in returning to martial arts, led to Steve finding school sports. He had previously played school sports and had found it somewhat enjoyable. The physical competition of sport couldn't fully replace martial arts training, but it was enough to direct Steve's anger and aggression, at least for now. For many years the martial arts were not revisited by Steve. He slowly began to forget about martial arts.

Steve focused on any and all sports he could at the new school. He participated in athletics and group sports excelling in some athletics events and had the potential to excel in the group sports. Unfortunately, the social hierarchy that existed with these new peers meant he could never truly excel in any group sport as Steve was towards the bottom of this social hierarchy. Whenever it appeared that he would have a chance to excel in sports a peer would take that opportunity away, and no teacher would do anything to stop them.

Despite this, Steve was slowly becoming content with sports. He was again being forced to be self-reliant. What other choice did he have? Steve's life appeared to reduce in chaos in this new location, at least compared to his early childhood environment. There was no standout teacher who supported him like his previous town, but the stability allowed Steve to pursue his intellect on his own. He drew from the positive experiences several teachers from his previous school had provided him. Something he had not thought about since the last time he was in a supportive classroom. The urge to fill his (not well understood) hole had reduced, or so he thought.

Steve decided he would try going to university and be the first one in his family to do so. Being the first to complete university would be a type of victory. He graduated school and focused just enough to get the minimum grades he needed. Once he graduated from high school, he applied for a university near his previous town. Officially to everyone else and consciously to Steve, he had to move towns as this university offered a better program.

Steve did not understand at the time, that moving towns was an excuse to escape his current environment. Why would he understand this when he thought he was content? It wouldn't be until many years later that he would finally understand that leaving this town and returning close to his first town was an escape. An unconscious urge to return to something that had less social hierarchy, had previously involved positive and supportive adults away from his family, and promised the potential to improve his intelligence.

Moving for Intellectual Pursuit?

Consciously, Steve moved to another town attempting to embrace his intelligence. Steve knew that he didn't want to ever return to the level of poverty and violence he had experienced as a child and felt that university could be the ticket.

The learning environment at the university was stimulating enough, and he initially enjoyed the challenge. However, the learning environment soon became boring, the lecturers were overtly closed minded while spruiking free thinking, and the learning became almost cumbersome. He met several positive peers which helped him to stay for a little longer, but even this wasn't enough to keep him there for long.

Steve found that his internal motivation was not enough to keep him at university. He had always thought of himself as driven but was slowly (but not consciously) experiencing that without the threat of violence or overt punishment, completing his goals was more difficult. This then encouraged Steve to forget about pursuing intellectual goals and instead return to something physical such as sport.

After several months of pursuing sport at the university, enjoying it but not excelling, this too became boring. He then chose to return to his original martial art while working random jobs. He was not sure what led him to do this, but there was something about the controlled violence, the channelling of his anger that neither sports nor books seemed to assist with. He returned to his first martial art and quickly began excelling again.

Again, he won tournaments locally and beyond. He was working just enough to cover the expenses of living as an adult and martial arts training. During his training, something unexpected happened. Steve met a girl through a mutual friend. This was unexpected surprise and even more unexpectedly things went well for a while. However, eventually the relationship didn't work out.

Not because the other person wasn't positive, they were great. There was just something not right. Steve did not understand why but knew she wasn't someone he could settle down with. He would later understand that this person whilst supportive, did not provide enough of a challenge. Steve's needs were almost oxymoronic; he needed support but also needed a challenge. He continued his training making it to his black belt and then became bored again.

Steve was confused, he had finally been able to choose to train where and when he wanted, he had the drive and had won the stuff, but now he felt unfocused. In hindsight it might have been because there was no environmental reason to channel his anger at this point in his life. He had made friends and even dating was a positive experience. He had tried to reframe the boredom as a positive. A sign that life was more than just violence. However, even this positive reframing and appreciation wasn't enough.

Eventually, after several months he did the only other thing he knew, he changed his environment. But keeping in his pattern of behaviours, he returned to the other environment he knew.

Returning

Steve eventually made the necessary plans to move. He said his goodbyes to people, had a going away event and then left.

He returned to his second environment. Returning home to his second environment from childhood slowly caused Steve's urge to train in martial arts to return. There wasn't anything overtly violent, there was only a couple of threats to his and his parent's life but to him this was within the normal. A family friend threatened to burn his family's house down for "opening their mouth with an opinion", and another person threatened murder with a syringe using her knowledge as a nurse.

This syringe threat might have stuck with Steve more than he thought.

Whatever the reason, his previous hole began to need filling again. As had always been the case for Steve, it wasn't an overnight thing. It was a slow buildup until he eventually went full speed to fulfil the urge. This time though, instead of returning to the one martial art he had previously trained in, Steve tried to fill his inner hole with lots of martial arts at once.

He did a bit of research into what options were available. For Steve it had to appear logical. He enjoyed watching movies with flowery martial arts moves and flips in the air, but training in these styles never appealed to him. The moves and the flips felt wasteful. Eventually he found several martial gyms teaching different but complimentary martial arts. He decided almost without realising that his life focus was now martial arts.

He worked to pay for training. The job itself didn't matter if the pay was enough. But he also wouldn't put up with bullying towards him. His life had shaped him so that he would refuse to allow bullying and discrimination against him. When jobs or management annoyed him or attempted to bully him, he quit and found another job that would help pay for training. This continued for several years. His life purpose was to work to pay for martial arts training.

He again began excelling in his training. Ideas of work and life balance were non-existent. In his attempts to fill whatever void or hole there was inside him, Steve began overcompensating. He would train in one very physical and brutal martial art, then run to the next martial art school to train in their very physical and brutal martial art. The training was taking its toll on Steve's body, but it was never enough. The need to train could not be fully satiated. The need to train became a form of an addiction and this began to overflow. He would train through injuries and punch through bloodied knuckles.

Instead of being teased for being crazy, his martial arts peers were supportive, and some were reportedly in awe. Steve's mental strength (as it appeared to his martial arts peers), was being celebrated by his peers. Steve still had no insight into mental health and no understanding of his social difficulties in life. He just knew it felt nice to have his hard work celebrated. This support would then increase his intensity in training.

The physical pain of training also helped to centre Steve. Chest pain meant he was stressed, but except for that, pain meant he was alive. Pain was a welcome experience, was the norm for Steve, it was comfortable.

Emotions too were not that relevant to Steve's experience or understanding of life. The only emotions Steve understood were anger and laughing. There were no other emotions that he knew or cared about knowing.

Martial arts training had become his fixation. Steve knew nothing of nutrition and rest. In this state, Steve only knew of one thing – hard work and working hard. His previous wit and intelligence had now once again, taken a backseat. If he did have any other life goals previously, these too had taken a backseat. He felt that his identity was that of a martial artist.

Building a Life

Returning to martial arts, especially to the extreme Steve was now training, had given Steve structure, purpose, confidence and a way to avoid other responsibilities in life. However, life is what happens when you are busy making plans, and after several years of this intense training Steve accidentally met a girl.

Stephanie was different to the other ladies he had met. Stephanie appeared to understand Steve and support Steve. She supported his training, but also gently encouraged other pursuits. She also provided stability.

It happened faster than Steve realised. Over the course of several months something changed inside of Steve. His fixation on training slowed until it eventually fell to a healthy level of exercise only. He began to settle down.

Whatever hole he had that was previously been filled with martial arts was now being filled by something else. He began building a life with Stephanie. Stephanie was not only a kind person but also offered Steve stability and support without the need for violence.

Steve and Stephanie worked hard, and with the support and stability provided by Stephanie, Steve was able to embrace his wit and intelligence again. Stephanie supported Steve's intellectual pursuits. Supporting Steve to complete entry level study and then later supported Steve to complete formal study at university. Steve still experienced difficulties sticking to one thing without the threat of violence. When Steve showed signs of wanting to quit, Stephanie was there to gently redirect and support him to finish.

Despite the several changes and side steps, Steve still managed to be the first in his family to complete university study.

Using his degree and the social networking skill he had been spent years improving, he found stable work in a new office job. His new job allowed him to educate and help people including doctors, vets, police officers, medical students and various other groups and individuals, to improve and manage their health-related difficulties.

Once Steve's employment had stabilised, he and Stephanie then, built a house and started a family.

Starting a family was something Steve had wanted and he knew he would struggle. He had learned that most people use the tools their parents and childhood environment had taught them to then raise their children. What tools did Steve have? He had learned the theory and tools at university, but under pressure would he be able to use these? His biggest fear was replicating the violence of his youth. Thankfully, Stephanie was there to support Steve and together they began raising several healthy, but very energetic children.

Steve was content. This time he was actually content. He and Stephanie and their family were living a very busy but enjoyable life. Their children were all very different, all had great qualities, and everything was as perfect as can be in real life. For eighteen years Steve had what he considered to be the perfect life for himself. But all good things must come to an end, so they say. Steve had already experienced this but had allowed himself to form open and emotional attachment to Stephanie and their children. He allowed himself to openly show the world that he had something outside himself that was important to him.

Unfortunately for Steve, he was about to find out again in the worse way possible, that anything no matter how important can be taken away. He was about to relearn that attachments no matter how positive, can open you up to damage.

The Day Good Things End

The day started like any other normal day. Stress in the morning ensuring his children have what they needed, ensuring that he and Stephanie are sorted for work, and ensuring that they have a loose plan for their afternoon.

Steve and Stephanie had a rule that when they were on the phone or one was leaving to go do something, that the conversations ended in "I love you". It was a silly thing to some people, but Steve was very rigid with this, and ensured he always said it, even if he was unhappy with a situation or if he and Stephanie were arguing.

Stephanie left for work early in the morning as she always did so that she could finish in time to pick up the children from school. Steve did the usual school drop-off and then went to work.

It was a very normal day, almost boringly normal. Steve was still at work while Stephanie picked up the children from school. Stephanie and their children were on their way to their sports and martial arts training. It is sunny and hot, with only a spattering of clouds. There is nothing whatsoever exceptional about this day.

Steve received a phone call while he was working and waited until after the shift had finished to return the call. It was from an unknown number, so Steve listened to the phone message. It was a call from the local police station. Steve had seen enough to know that these types of phone calls were rarely good news. He tried calling Stephanie, but she didn't answer. This didn't mean the worse was true, because she sometimes had her phone on silent because the sporting and martial arts locations made it difficult to hear anyone on the phone.

But what if it was the worse news? Steve began feeling anxious. This was an odd feeling for Steve, but one that arrived once he had enough in life outside himself, to care about. He eventually called the local police station back. They asked Steve to attend the local station and strongly suggest that Steve bring a close friend or family member. Steve had a lot of questions, but the officer politely explained that they would answer them all when Steve arrived. The police officer on the phone wouldn't say anything more.

Steve called his one close friend, but they didn't answer, obviously still at work. He thought about calling his family but didn't know if that would be helpful. He tried his friend one more time and again no answer. He decided to swallow the vomit that had now entered his mouth and drove himself to the police station. He arrived in record time. He must have been driving on autopilot and hoped that he hadn't gone through any red lights or stop signs.

He found a close carpark, not bothering to pay the parking metre as he had more important things on his mind. He half ran and half walked to the station door. He held back tears and advised the officer at the front desk who he was and that he had received a phone call. The officer then called officer Jerry who then requested that Steve follow him from the hallway into one of their rooms.

The silence in the station was deafening as they walked towards the room. Jerry hadn't said anything. Through his job, Steve had previously helped police officers at the station one of whom was Jerry. So, for Jerry to be silent, something must have been wrong.

Jerry closed the door and told Steve the worse news. Steve's family had been killed in a motor vehicle collision. Steve thought he hadn't heard officer Jerry correctly. He asks the officer to repeat. Again, Jerry stated that Steve's family had been killed in a motor vehicle collision.

Steve couldn't hold back his tears anymore. Through his crying he asked for a bucket and then emptied the contents of his stomach into the bucket. His chest pain that he previously only experienced relating to emotions he didn't understand, hit him at once. He tried to stand but he found that his body would not allow him to maintain his stance and he collapsed to the floor. He lay on the floor with his feet elevated for quite some time.

Eventually, Steve asks the question "are you sure"? It sounded like a silly question, but Steve was hoping that someone had made an error. Jerry replied that they were confident it was Steve's family as they used Stephanie's phone to get Steve's number. Steve wanted more answers, he asked if they knew how it happened. All

Jerry could say was that a car was driving and appeared to drive through a red light. Steve pressed Jerry for more information. Jerry tried to choose his words carefully, trying not to be too descriptive. He then continued with saying that the driver of the other vehicle attempted to swerve after the red light but was driving too fast and caused the vehicle that contained Steve's family to become damaged, killing them instantly.

Steve remained on the floor and asked for some water. Several minutes passed while Jerry went and filled a bottle of water for Steve. Once he received the bottle of water, he asked Jerry if he could be left alone for a time. Since it wasn't overly busy in the station, Jerry agreed and told Steve he would return in fifteen minutes.

His world would never be the same again. Steve lay on the cold floor, his body and mind in a state of shock and a form of numbness. Comfort no longer seemed important. The details Jerry had provided him were not the whole picture. He wanted to know more but also knew Jerry wouldn't be allowed to tell him too much. With no one left to care for, at least not to the level he had just lost, what would he do? The question stayed in Steve's head for several minutes until he found the energy required to be able to move.

Eventually, Steve sat up and finished the bottle of water. Jerry returned a minute later and asked if Steve was ready to continue through the difficult process of identifying photos of the deceased, signing paperwork and so forth.

Steve reluctantly agreed. The photos of the accident were brought into the room and this caused Steve to cry uncontrollably while confirming the identities. He stared at the photos through his tears, until the images were burned into his brain. Every blink felt like a still shot of what was just shown to him.

Fifteen minutes passed with Steve crying the entire time. Eventually he was able to stop crying enough so that he could complete the required paperwork with Jerry's assistance.

He asked Jerry if they could inform Stephanie's family members while Steve was in the room. Possibly because of how they knew each other, or possibly because it had been a slow day apart from Steve's current situation, but whatever the reason Jerry agreed. He called Stephanie's other next of kin and after many tears the family member and Jerry organised for someone to pick Steve up because he was too weak to drive.

Nearing the time of the organised pickup, Jerry walked Steve outside of the station. Once they were far enough away, Jerry told Steve some details that would cost him his job if anyone found out.

Finding Out Who

Steve had now just relearned a lesson he had began to forget 'life is pain'. Pain had previously given Steve clarity, drive and direction. Through positive life experiences, Steve had begun to believe that he could live a life of clarity and enjoyment without serious pain. He had begun to believe that there was more to life than fighting and survival. That belief had now dissipated very abruptly and violently.

Jerry approached Steve, leant in towards Steve, and half whispered to Steve "off the record, we know who was driving the other car. Again, I shouldn't be telling you this, but it was a person known as Keres and he had his girlfriend in the car with him. Legally we can't touch him because he has a very powerful lawyer and is a very famous fighter, and every time we have tried to charge him with a crime, he has successfully counter sued us. I'm telling you this, not to direct you to do something stupid, but so that it might help you find some closure".

A small part of Jerry instantly regretted telling Steve as much information as he did. But his own positive emotions towards Steve and his own negative emotions towards Keres, might have influenced his urge to share.

Steve had vaguely heard about this person named Keres before and had seen him on television. He had never watched any of Keres' fights, but from what he had seen on the news, Keres seemed to love the fame, something which made Steve pay even less attention. Now Steve had understood Keres through a different lens.

Keres was no longer just another famous person who Steve couldn't stand. Keres was now something more to Steve. Even if Keres didn't know it yet, Steve and Keres' futures were now connected. They would stay connected until Steve found the appropriate ending.

Steve thanked Jerry for his support knowing that Jerry wasn't supposed to tell him that information. Steve reassured Jerry that this news should help him find peace eventually even though he knew that this was not true.

Stephanie's family member picked Steve up from the station and drove him home. Steve left the car at the station and after several days it was eventually towed.

The days that followed the horrible news were a blur. Stephanie's family helped Steve to organise the funeral and several fruit trees were planted in memory of Stephanie and their children.

Steve didn't sleep much. He tried using the tools he had used professionally to help other people sleep, but they were ineffectual for Steve. He thought about using alcohol and drugs but knew this would only make him worse. He then returned to what had always worked for him as a child, playing loud angry music into his headphones while starring at the ceiling fan on the highest speed until his eyes were forced to close. This seemed to work, at least for a period.

Depression

Steve didn't want to pick his car up because he knew he would have to see the children's car seats. But he eventually organised a friend to pick up the car from the impound lot. The friend then drove the car back to Steve's and stayed for a chat.

The conversation didn't involve much talking, mostly crying on Steve's end. Eventually, Steve thanked the friend and the friend headed to work.

After several days of ordering food deliveries to the house, Steve built up enough energy to go to his car. Through tears, he removed the child seats and placed them in the respective bedrooms. After falling down multiple times from the weight of emotion, Steve closed the bedroom doors and locked the car.

He then lumbered to his bedroom and collapsed on the bed. Exhausted from emotion and from his poor sleep. Steve slept for two days. After the two-day sleep, Steve avoided most of the house and purposely used tunnel vision to avoid looking at the photos of his family that still covered most walls.

His friends, family and Stephanie's family had continued to visit Steve for several weeks until they eventually had to return to their own lives and responsibilities. During the blur of organising the funeral and other arrangements, Steve had also quit his job. Management was supportive and promised him a position there in the future should he wish to return.

Once the visitors stopped coming Steve had no reason to get out of bed. His loss had slowly turned to severe depression. He ate, drunk and slept in the same areas of his house every day, the kitchen, bedroom and bathroom. Steve was slowly slipping towards complete emptiness.

Slowly, even eating became difficult. Where before he would eat four or five meals a day, organised around a busy and fulfilling life, he now struggled to eat one. He didn't exercise, didn't read, didn't play any consoles games, he had no routine. He woke at random times, eventually rolled out of bed with his bladder and bowel needs the only motivator. On some days he would stay on the toilet staring at the bathroom cupboard until his legs were so numb that when he attempted to stand, he would fall.

He would then crawl to the kitchen, use the handles to pull himself up, and either eat what was there or order food to his door. He slowly stopped answering the door and instead would wait until it was delivered to his front porch to collect it. Because of the life insurance from Stephanie's death, he didn't need to work. He could remain in his hole in an ongoing cycle where days and nights merged into one.

Occasionally he allowed himself to look up from the floor and see the walls with photos, or pay attention to the furniture, or even look towards his children's bedrooms, but this only hurt him more. He didn't want to take the photos down and didn't want to touch any of the furniture. A part of him still believed that by having the photos on the wall and everything where it was, he would not be alone.

As his depression begun to worsen, even the bladder and bowel motivation reduced. The lack of food and the ease of laying a towel down, meant he slowly remained in bed longer and longer.

His room stunk but Steve did not notice this foul body odour stench that would have been noticeable for anyone with an average sense of smell. Eventually though something odd would happen, that would redirect his life again. As if his life was driven by an invisible dice roll.

Cupboard

Steve had lived in silence for so long that even the sound of him breathing felt intrusive. Days bled together into a single mass of stillness and stale air. He rarely ventured beyond the hallway, rarely opened a window, rarely acknowledged the sun.

His house that was once filled with noise, laughter, arguments, and the background hum of life, had since become an echo chamber of silence and Steve had let it.

On an otherwise unremarkable morning, Steve felt something different. Not energy. Not hope. Just a small, irritating urge. An impulse to do something. Steve hadn't felt this urge for several months.

He tried to ignore it.

He lay on the bed longer. Scrolled on his phone, wasted time scrolling but not really looking, reading or absorbing information from the random articles. He stared at the ceiling fan hoping it would dry his eyes out to help him go to sleep despite the time of day. He closed his eyes, hoping the day would disappear like all the others. But the urge didn't dissipate, it grew. It wasn't loud. It wasn't emotional. It just pressed at him, like a tap on the shoulder from someone who refuses to be ignored.

After attempts to ignore the urge failed, he listened to the urge to clean his clothing cupboard. He had no idea why he had this sudden urge but after several hours, he stopped fighting the urge and mustered the strength to clean the cupboard. At first, he just stood there, staring, he went to walk backwards away from the cupboard, but something internally was stopping him.

Before cleaning the cupboard, he decided to have a shower perhaps the first shower he had had for at least a month. Once he decided to have a shower, he saw his face and body for the first time in a long time, a shadow of his former self. He was never massive, but he used to be disciplined and strong, now he looked gaunt and shaggy. He used the electric shaver Stephanie had previously bought him to shave his face and then chose to have a shower. He accidently nicked his skin several times but felt nothing as the blood hit the sink below. Showering and shaving gave him enough energy to go to the clothing cupboard with at least a small amount of intent.

Eventually, he began pulling clothes out. He dropped them onto the bed in a messy heap. He paused at Stephanie's clothing. Then carefully worked around her clothing as not to disturb it. He continued throwing his clothing out of the cupboard. He still hadn't gone anywhere near his children's bedrooms. They had been untouched since his friends and family stopped visiting to return to their normal lives.

He grabbed items from his cupboard and threw them onto the bed. Eventually the smaller piles merged into one large pile taking up most the space on the bed. As he threw the last pile of clothing onto the bed something fell off the bed and onto the floor.

He walked to the side of the bed. He leant down and picked it up. The texture was familiar. It is one of his old martial arts uniforms. Steve began crying. This wasn't anything new for Steve since his family had been killed, or as he saw it, murdered. But this crying felt different, unlike the hollow, empty grief that had consumed him for months. This crying had a different intensity, a different rhythm to it. It was sharper, angrier, more alive even.

It shook something loose inside him. He held the uniform to his chest. Pressed his forehead into it. Somatic memories flooded his body until he felt it easier to lay on top of the clothing pile than to stand. He began remembering his teachers, his tournaments, the supportive people, the violence, and his change from angry child to martial artist to family man.

Until he met Stephanie, martial arts training was the key positive, it had saved him from drowning in circumstances far bigger than himself and beyond his control.

It was then, with the uniform pressed against his chest, breath shaking, tears falling, that he acknowledged the shift within. Something inside him had turned. He did not know if this was for better or worse, and he did not care. He just knew that something was different.

Mongrel Rebirth

Rebirth rarely arrived with inspiration or clarity or a sudden burst of motivation. It often came from the negative or ugly places such as grief, or from rage buried beneath months of numbness.

With his old Gi still in hand, he rolled off the clothing pile and chose to listen to the radio instead of the recent silence or angry music, he had become accustomed to.

While listening to the radio and crying even more at certain songs that reminded him of the good times with his family, he heard a gambling add that mentioned the big martial arts fight involving the reigning champion Keres and the contender.

Something inside Steve changes. Sadness is replaced with focus. The focus is fuelled by a version of something he hasn't experienced since his childhood, the feeling of seeking vengeance. Even his intense martial arts training before he met Stephanie was different to what he felt as a child. But this time, the fuel felt more potent than his childhood fuel. It was like his previous inner mongrel that he used as a child had arisen. His inner mongrel that was fuelled by surviving instability, fuelled by violence, fuelled by never accepting defeat. But this was unfiltered. Unfiltered by life's social needs, unfiltered by the need to fit in anywhere, it was straight mongrel fermented with something else.

A part of him had been concerned about the mongrel's return. A part of him had wanted an excuse for the mongrel. None of him wanted to lose his family as payment for the unfiltered mongrel.

He searched online looking for a training gym that will best suit his goals. He didn't want to return to his previous training gyms as there were still too connected to Stephanie and his family. He wanted to find training gyms that focused on fighting and had nothing to do with his family. After shortlisting several gyms, he left the house to visit them.

Steve spoke with several training gyms and told them of his goals to be a professional fighter. Some instructors laughed, given his almost gaunt shape. But Steve was not deterred. He eventually found a gym with several coaches who were willing to help him.

Steve agreed to their terms and then began their training, with his inner mongrel unlocked again. The training gave him focus, it made him feel in control. It removed the feelings of powerlessness. It changed the type of numbness he was experiencing. This numbness changed from feeling emotionally numb, to being mentally numb to fear, not caring about being hurt. This type of numbness was preferred to the emptiness.

He trained at the gym with several coaches and excelled as he had in the past with the mongrel rage making up for his older age and smaller frame. This time though, he put a lot of effort into ensuring he ate enough food, but he didn't track calories or weight, that's what his coaches were being paid for. Within a month his physique has changed from the gaunt figure he saw in the mirror before cleaning his cupboard to his previous physically healthy self.

Steve asked for some two-on-one training so that he could sharpen his skills. Initially several of the younger fighters were more than happy to engage in the request, but eventually the volunteers stopped. He wasn't training for sport, fun, fitness or with the intent to heal. He was training to get a chance at revenge. He was training to avenge his family.

He trained well at the local gym and had several unofficial fights with much younger fighters. On paper at least, he won those easily, walking towards the punches, kicks and elbows as he closed distance to deliver his own strikes. Steve won these organised unofficial fights by knockout.

After knocking people out at sparring and winning the fights without breaking a sweat he then had his first recognised fight. This fighter was an up-and-coming fighter who had his own goals of making it in the sport. This wasn't a sport for Steve as the fighter would soon find out. The younger fighter was quickly whelmed by Steve's approach. Steve won the fight by knockout but received some damage because of his lack of care. His fight coach lectured him and made some good points, enough for Steve to listen.

If Steve was to succeed in the big-time fights against properly trained fighters, who will often be younger than he, Steve needed to be better and take less damage.

Steve knew the coach was correct. If Steve was to meet Keres, then the quickest way was through fighting success. This meant he would need to be successful enough to be invited into the same room as Keres and not be too broken when that invitation arrived.

Steve had disengaged from his friends, family and Stephanie's family over the last several months and been focusing on fighting. They kind of understood. They understood that the fighting helped Steve get out of the house and into the world again. They didn't understand what his intentions or goals were. They said nothing, at least to his face.

Fighting Rise

The rise didn't happen as quickly as Steve liked but it did happen. He knew that we were all shaped by our history and that if we could channel and redirect negative experiences, we could use it as fuel to achieve. Steve had been given more fuel to use.

Steve trained a lot more, this time focusing on closing distance without taking damage. He trained hard at the gym, sparring anyone who would dare enter the ring with him regardless of their size or age. Initially, his coach gave him people his size to spar. Eventually, though, only the larger people in the gym wanted to enter the sparring ring, often hoping they would teach Steve a lesson.

Pain had become a familiar feeling. What was pain but weakness leaving the body? When Steve trained, he didn't think, he didn't feel, he was in the zone. He was there to get better as a fighter so he could finish what was started by Keres.

He continued eating healthier and eating a lot more than did in his youth. He watched hundreds of hours of fights, fixated on Keres's fights as well as any similar fighters. While watching the fights he broke down how they moved, how they closed and changed distance. A part of his intellect was still there in the background, which prompted him to ask a math lecturer to breakdown fight videos, with a strong focus on Keres and his behaviours in the ring.

Steve had previously helped this math lecturer and knew their strength with data analysis and their strong interest in sport, especially combat sport. Steve had hoped that with this knowledge, it would improve his efficiency in the ring.

His daily routine revolved around fighting and training. Within eighteen months of eating, sleeping, training and fighting he finally received a shot in the undercard. After eighteen fights for eighteen wins Steve was given a chance.

The chance came to Steve through his coach. Steve fought a brutal two round fight where Steve threw almost everything at his opponent, but his opponent wouldn't fall. Towards the end of the fight, he was given several warnings about striking illegal targets. This didn't bother Steve; it only encouraged him to finish the fight quickly. Five seconds from the end of the second round he was able to land the knockout blow. When Steve landed an inside thigh kick and caused his opponent to buckle, it easier for Steve's elbow to hit the temple of his opponent.

Steve was later told by his coach, that his opponent was using this fight as recognition for the upcoming Undercard spot. Since Steve won, convincingly (at least on paper), the fight organisation offered Steve the spot instead.

The coach told Steve that if he accepted the offer, he would be one step closer to officially making it to the big time. Steve had never shared what his end goal was, not exactly. He had allowed his coaches to fill the gaps between his vague language and his intense training. They had assumed he wanted to make it in the big time and become famous, or become one of the oldest debut fighters, or something like that. He never corrected them.

Steve asked his coach to accept, and Steve was officially sent the invitation for the Undercard fight for six weeks' time. After Steve's last fight, it highlighted a few things that Steve still needed to work on. Specifically, around avoiding damage and making his strikes count.

Steve then trained as intensely as his coaches allowed. Some sessions his coaches had to force him to have a break, or reduce his workload, other times they had to remind Steve to eat more or even go home to sleep. Steve was taking this opportunity very seriously.

The six weeks passed in what felt like one. He had been training intensely physically and when he wasn't sleeping, eating or training, he was watching footage and speaking with the math lecturer. He was going to win, not try, but win.

Undercard and Beyond

Steve didn't mind that he was only on the undercard and not yet fighting Keres. He knew that if he won the Undercard, it would get him closer to Keres.

The night of Steve's first big fight arrived. He noticed how many people were there, not for him, but there to watch the fighting, hoping for their favourite to win by knockout. The fighter's room smelled the same as any training gym, sweaty with the strong smell of Thai oil in the air. The noise was the only difference.

Every fighter had their own entry song, often an aggressive or energetic song that helped get the fighter pumped.

When Steve's time came to do the long walk to the ring he didn't choose his angry music. He didn't choose any form of uplifting music like most of the fighters. His song choice was his wedding song. He hadn't told his choice to his coaches until the very last second and despite their arguments, Steve refused to budge.

The announcer spoke and called through the speakers "Steve". As the announcer was doing his calling, Steve's music choice began. The announcer found it difficult to continue speaking for several seconds as he was trying to hold back laughter. Most of the crowd went silent and then eventually began to laugh at Steve but he took no notice.

The wedding song helped fuel his mongrel rage. He felt sorry for his opponent in a way, but his opponent was a stepping stone to get to Keres. Steve entered the fight ring, completed the fight pleasantries and as soon as the fight officially started, after the touching of the gloves, he delivered a push kick towards the opponent, heel first into their nose. The opposing fighter was knocked out. The crowd was again silent for a second or two, then they cheered for Steve.

Steve bowed. The bow hadn't been practiced, but something within told him it was the right thing to do. He wanted to decline the interview but realised that he could use this attention to help him get a fight with Keres. He hoped that if he called Keres out, it would draw the attention of the fight organisers, and this might provide Steve the opportunity earlier.

Steve spoke with the commentator thanking the crowd. He then explained that his odd song choice was inspired by his late wife and despite the pacing of the song, it helped provide focus and motivation. Steve then called out Keres, saying that he understood he is still a nobody in the fight world, but he would love to ensure everyone forgot about Keres as soon as possible. Steve also shared that he hated everything that Keres represented and was happy to erase his name from the fight logs.

Following his quick knockout, odd song entrance, and even bolder interview, the news was drawn towards the situation and outcome. Various television channels and talk shows that don't normally speak about professional fighters shared snippets of the entrance song and the bold interview. Steve went viral online within hours. None of this Steve paid attention to as he had no social media and didn't watch any entertainment that wasn't useful for his fighting.

Steve completed several Undercard fights, each time he won and delivered a variation of his speech calling out Keres. Several Undercard fights later and Steve was given a chance to prove his worth. Every Undercard began the same for Steve – his wedding song is his entrance song; the crowd laughs then cheers. Every Undercard fight ends the same for Steve – he enters the rings, does the pleasantries then finds very efficient ways to knock the opponent out.

Despite some negative opinions from fellow fighters who are jealous at the attention Steve was receiving, he was eventually given an opportunity to fight against Bob. The fight world was informed that if Steve defeated Bob in the fight, he would have a *chance* to fight Keres for the title belt. If Steve defeated Bob quickly, the fight organisers would *guarantee* Steve's next fight was a title fight against Keres.

Steve was pleased with this news. If he defeated Bob quickly, he would be able to legally go against the person who killed his family. As he had done now for what felt like a lifetime, he did his homework on the upcoming fight. He watched his opponent's last twenty fights, spoke with the math lecturer, and noticed that Bob loved to be aggressive and close distance as quickly as possible, often with aerial attacks.

Steve and his coaches focused on being prepared for Bob. His focus and intensity was there, and as has been a pattern, his coaches were there to ensure Steve didn't "overdo it". In Steve's mind there was no longer such a thing as "over doing it", but he listened to the coaches as he didn't want to lose his one shot.

Steve entered the ring with the intention of exploiting Bob's tactics to win the fight as quickly as possible.

The Fight Conspiracy

Steve's training and lessons learned in the ring had continued to shape him in ways he had not yet realised. His body had become sharper, his fight IQ had improved, and he had earned the respect of many of the younger fighters. His childhood hyperawareness and life's lessons had helped him to improve a greater than expected rate.

The fight night finally arrived. Several minutes before the big fight his coach pulled him aside. The coach had heard rumours that very powerful people wanted to see Steve lose the fight. Steve's response did not please the coach, and he asked Steve if there was any chance, he would consider faking an injury and losing the fight. The coach said it wasn't ideal, but it would be the safest choice of action for Steve. Steve did not respond. He stood up and walked towards the entrance.

Steve's entrance song played. The crowd no longer laughed first, they went straight into a cheer. Steve went through the pattern of walking around the ring, listening to the referee and doing the fight pleasantries. The news his coach had just given him only fuelled Steve's urge to win further. Steve did not respond well to threats or bullies no matter how powerful the people were supposed to be.

The fight began as Steve expected. Bob attempted to rush Steve and attempted an aerial kick, potentially attempting to knock Steve out in one kick. Steve had prepared for this. He had watched videos, paid the math lecturer to analyse the patterns, and listened to his coaches about how to negate this. Expecting Bob's type of attack, Steve quickly and efficiently changed the angle and chopped low on Bob's rear leg as it was leaving the ground. The timing was perfect.

Just as Bob was leaving the ground to attack Steve at speed, his leg was taken out. This caused Bob to become almost horizontal exposing his liver and spine to Steve.

Steve successfully performed an axe kick to Bob's liver as Bob was falling to the ground, which caused Bob immense pain based on his odd scream. Bob tried to get off the ground but was struggling too much and eventually just stayed on the ground. Steve's kick and Bob landing had all but ensured a victory for Steve. The fight should have been over. Steve didn't want to kill Bob, he just needed to win quickly so he yelled at the referee to call the fight, but the ref didn't listen.

Bob was still on the ground as Steve was yelling at the referee. The referee appeared confused. Steve had quickly begun to realise that the fight must have been fixed as his coach had suggested, and that he wasn't supposed to win.

Seeing the referee refuse to stop the fight, Steve walked around the ring for several seconds. He then decided to bend down on the mat and tap it three times, essentially throwing the fight and taking the loss. The result was what the powerful people wanted and unfortunately for Steve, he had just given it to them, but this wasn't the end. Not for Steve. It was only the end of the fight. Steve still had goals.

Steve then left the ring as the crowd was largely silent. Several people in the crowd were cheering, a couple were booing, but overall, the silence was almost deafening. Even the commentators were left shocked and didn't know what they had just witnessed.

Steve then agreed to hold a press conference. Steve openly shared his conspiracy that he thought that the fight was fixed. He openly shared what his coach had been told by a mysterious person, and he then shared exactly why

Bob needed medical attention, and why the referee should have called the fight. He then spoke to the journalists listening and told them that he didn't want to kill Bob since "he only killed people he didn't like, hypothetically speaking of course".

He explained he felt he had to take the loss as it was the morally right thing to do. He wished Bob and his family all the best. He then told the journalists that he would have to take three months away from the fighting sport so he could reassess if the fighting body was able to be trusted again and to reassess his goals. He reported that he would not pursue legal action at this time, but if he was pressured by the organisation, then he might.

As Steve entered the dressing rooms, some of the younger fighters thanked him. His coaches did not. They didn't want Steve to take time away, not when he was so close. They also were unhappy for being openly pulled into the conspiracy, not matter how true. They tried to in vain to change Steve's mind about taking time off. But to no avail. Steve had made his mind up and there was nothing anyone could do to change it.

Search for Keres

Steve now had to find the original perpetrator the hard way. Doing the right thing by Bob meant that he would not get a title shot against Keres. This meant he would have to find Keres the hard way. By this time, Steve had watched hundreds of hours of Keres fighting and had also watched some social medial videos of Keres showing off.

This helped Steve to understand Keres a little better. It helped Steve to understand that Keres enjoyed being known as "showy", which meant he should be easier to track. Steve felt he could use this information to help him find Keres quickly.

After several weeks of following reports, tracking Keres' known associates and other social media research, Steve had theorised and mapped what Keres's routine was. He felt he knew where Keres should be and decided to pursue his own justice. He wanted to avenge his family but also didn't want to be caught. Steve redirected his mongrel rage from fighting and conditioning his body, to fuelling and directing his intelligence.

It didn't happen quickly. Steve had just spent many months channelling his mongrel into physical training, and now he needed to use it for intellectual pursuits. Instead of eight hours at a gym, Steve watched many hours studying Keres, and many worth of videos on the internet studying, chemistry videos, fungi and insect paralysis videos, and then became heavily focused on autoimmune diseases that cause paralysis.

Even though he wasn't exercising as intensely as he previously did, he maintained some exercise at home to help keep his mind and body sharp. He read several medical textbooks that discussed the similarities between autoimmune disease responses, paralysis and white blood cell counts in blood tests. He learned how courts used blood tests to look for clues. He was ready for the next step.

After all the reading and watching videos, Steve believed he had a good enough knowledge base to begin construction. He had concocted what he felt to be an ingenious plan that involved killing Keres without it being traced. After he felt he understood how to make a lethal paralytic chemically, he worked towards problem solving how he would deliver the paralytic substance in practice.

He didn't like guns but understood they might be a good way to distribute the paralysis poison. He then thought about dart guns. With a lot of effort, he was able to remember a person he had previously helped, who now worked as a vet. The people he had helped in what felt like a lifetime ago, had ways they could assist Steve in achieving his goal.

He travelled to the vet location and asked to speak to his previous client, who was the main vet at the practice. Steve had created a cover story that would ethically allow his previous client to assist him with any dart gun related questions. He spoke with the vet about farm animals and if dart guns could be useful. After the vet and Steve discussed how best to use a dart gun especially on animals who have high muscle density, Steve purchased the dart gun and several darts, paid for in cash. Once home, Steve emptied the liquid from the darts and began testing different paralytic combinations made from readily available fungi and insect venom.

Previously Steve hated the idea of testing products on animals, but he now needed to test his product. He decided that since mice were cheap and easy to find or purchase, he would have to perfect his paralytic on mice. Eventually, after testing it on several mice that he purchased from a pet store, he felt he had perfected a concoction. A nice present to give Keres, for all that he had done to Steve.

Keres Confrontation

After a week of waiting for Keres to follow his routine Steve spotted him in the parking lot. Normally Keres didn't travel anywhere without an entourage or woman by his side, with the only exception being when his favourite sports team was playing. Steve had been counting on this, waiting for the moment that Keres would be the most vulnerable. Perhaps this was the "real" Keres who just wanted to enjoy his sports team without wearing a mask.

Whatever the reason, Keres was now leaving the sports bar alone. Keres left the bar early that day as his sports team was losing by a lot, with not much chance of coming back. Steve watched from a short distance, enough to see and talk to a person, but not to close that they can hit you or hug you. Keres approached his car and opened his door belonging to his very expensive electric vehicle. Steve called out to him "Keres if I may have a word".

Keres didn't see Steve at first. He was drunk and sad for his sports team's effort. He heard Steve first then stopped to get a proper look at Steve as he staggered slightly to the right. He then realised who Steve was and laughed at him for throwing a fight and giving up a shot at taking the title.

Instead of replying to what Keres was saying, Steve instead yelled his deceased family's names back to Keres. This confused Keres and he replied, "are you drunk or are you high, yelling out random names". Steve then helped Keres understand the context by giving him the date and time of the car incident. It took several minutes for Keres to understand what this meant, he was drunk and he was used to his lawyers clearing his name. With some prompting from Steve, Keres eventually worked out what Steve was talking about.

Keres's face quickly turned from annoyance to anger. Keres then starts insulting Steve and saying his lawyers would have a field day with Steve again, if he tried anything silly. Steve ignored these empty threats. He then pulled out his dart gun. Keres initially started backing down when he saw what he thought was a gun. However, Keres then realises that it is just a toy gun or dart gun and starts taunting Steve again.

Keres then says to Steve "you can't even intimidate correctly, no wonder you have to finish your fights quickly, before your opponent knows how full of hot air you are". Steve says nothing in reply. He just smiles. He takes several steps towards Keres and shoots Keres in the chest. Keres initially is stunned but then doesn't feel anything happen.

Keres is about to laugh at Steve again, perhaps with the intention of taunting Steve some more, but he then begins to lose control of his legs. His body slowly begins sliding from an upright position to crumbling beneath him. Keres tries to grab his door to hold himself upright.

While this was happening, Steve had continued calmly walking towards Keres. Just as Steve was within kicking distance, Keres's arms slipped off the door, exposing his neck to the edge of the very sharp door frame. Luckily for Steve and unluckily for Keres, Keres' car had a well-known issue, an issue Keres was about to experience. Steve performed potentially his most aggressive front kick ever, with his heel. The door slams against Keres's body and Keres neck breaks, partially beheading Keres with the sharp edges of his vehicle's door. Steve then removes the dart carefully to leave no evidence.

Steve is both horrified and relieved. Steve had heard that this specific vehicle make and model had very sharp edges and had been used in demonstrations to cut carrots, but he never believed those videos, until now. He was horrified that Keres's neck broke so easily and that Keres's head was still barely attached.

Thankfully, for Steve, everyone else at the bar where Keres's car was parked near, had been inside listening to the sports. Everyone at the bar had been making so much noise that they didn't hear the altercation. Steve was relieved that to the best of his knowledge no one saw what he had just done.

Steve forgot to check for street cameras. He had been solely focused on his revenge. Thankfully, for Steve, he had a lucky break. There were two sets of street cameras nearby, but only one was working. The broken street camera would normally have seen exactly what had just occurred between Steve and Keres as it was normally used specifically for the carpark. Steve had caught a break.

Steve thought to himself "fitting really, that a person who craved attention died with no witnesses, except for a broken camera". Steve was also relieved that his revenge mission had been a success. He was still filled with adrenaline and decided to drive back home, then go for a run. He couldn't sleep much that night. However, despite his poor sleep, Steve woke feeling lighter, almost refreshed, and he decided to go to the last restaurant he and his family had gone to all that time ago.

With the death of Keres, Steve felt he might be ready to start processing his loss but was unsure where to start.

A day later after somebody found the body and called the police, the news and fight community were buzzing about the death of a fight legend. Theories abound about why and how Keres died. Steve ignored all of this.

Now What

Steve had begun refocusing on fighting. He tried to return to training and fighting at several of his regular training gyms as if nothing had happened. However, something fundamental to his fighting was missing and the coaches feedback was all the same.

The coaches shouted at Steve "Move forward!", "You're hesitating!", "Where's the pressure, close the distance'. His gym trainers kept telling Steve he now lacked the drive to move forward towards his opponents. They all thought it was connected to his last fight with Bob where Steve had accused the fight organisation of fixing a fight. They all thought that Steve had been humiliated, they thought that the stress of the fight world might have gotten to him.

No matter how hard Steve tried to focus on fighting, he couldn't, he didn't have any drive to compete. There was no longer a need to be better at fighting as his goal had been completed. He had no mongrel fuel left. It was spent. It was an odd feeling. He had relied on the mongrel as a child, and then he had relied on it after his family were murdered. Since he avenged his family though, he couldn't find it, no matter how hard he tried. He still felt emptiness, but it felt different somehow.

Despite this, the fight organisation tried offering Steve another fight. Steve felt like they wanted to offer Steve another fight to protect themselves legally.

They promised Steve a different referee and promised Steve that he could even choose his opponent. When bribes failed the fight organisation tried threats. They then tried threatening Steve to honour his contract or risk losing the remaining money from his sponsorship.

Steve never did respond well with threats, he didn't need money, he didn't care for fame, there was nothing that Steve could think that would make him fight again. Steve continued to decline the fights and eventually held another press conference, which some of his coaches felt was the right thing to do given his current difficulty in the ring. Not many news channels were interested as they had moved on to other fighters and other stories, but the two local news stations agreed to the press conference.

Steve didn't mind that there would be a small audience, he just wanted to get on the front foot with this fight stuff so he could hopefully do something else. He wasn't sure what that was, but he felt this was a first step.

When the interview began Steve didn't warm up to this point. He started the interview with the social pleasantries and then formally announced his retirement from fighting. He also then shared how the fight organisation had attempted to force him into fighting again, showing evidence of phone calls, emails, letters and voice messages. Steve shared how they had threatened to ensure Steve would lose his sponsorship money if he didn't fight.

Steve shared that he didn't care about the money or fame. He answered questions and then finished with "In the last several years I have achieved everything I wanted to achieve and more. I have met all my goals and am now ready to focus on rebuilding my life. Thank you for your time".

After the interview was wrapped up Steve said goodbye to his coaches and some of his fight peers. He thanked his coaches for their effort and guidance and wished them well. One question kept being asked to Steve "what will he do now", "Now What?". The question continued rattling around his head while he tried to sleep.

Rebuild my life, into what, how? Now
What?

Police and Keres

Since the death of Keres, the police had been searching everywhere for evidence. The official story was simple – that Keres was a victim of a car robbery gone wrong, a tragedy that no one could have foreseen. However, many people including most of the police service did not believe this.

Keres wasn't just any man, he was The Man. He was showy, had a posse, had as many women as he wanted. Many of the officers followed the results of the fights and as such they knew how well Keres could protect himself, at least in the ring. There was also no sign of gun shots, stab wounds or even bruising except where the door impacted Keres' neck. Anyone especially police officers, would expect at least some bruising from a physical altercation.

Toxicology only showed elevated levels of alcohol and white blood cells, so there was no evidence of poison. There was no explanation as to why or how someone would be able to easily kill Keres. Even a drunk Keres would not have been an easy target for the average would be criminal. A few officers thought the white blood cell count being high was odd, but no one had enough knowledge about that stuff to make sense of why they felt it was odd, so they moved on.

The police had been searching for eyewitnesses, especially since the bar was relatively close by. However, all people questioned said a similar thing, they had been watching the sports and didn't see or hear anything.

One of the junior officers suggested looking deeper into Keres' fight opponents to see if there was any personal motive that hadn't showed up yet. They were given permission to do so and after several months, the officer had found nothing. As he went to inform his boss of this, he noticed that a colleague was looking especially sombre.

The officer asked what was wrong and his colleague replied that he had recently witnessed a car accident that looked personal and that the accident had happened near their house.

The junior officer quickly had an idea. Instead of running to his boss' office, he returned to his own. He had been focusing on fighters specifically, but what if Keres in his showy bravado had pissed off a civilian. It wouldn't explain how the civilian killed Keres, but it would give motive.

The junior officer returned to his search with a renewed focus. He delved through Keres' personal life and sure enough there were a lot of times where Keres' legal team helped him get away with stuff. The junior officer had heard about this type of story before but hadn't experienced it yet in his work. This officer was driven and details focused. He reread everything in the Keres file.

He noticed that lots of the legal issues Keres' legal team had helped him with didn't seem like enough motive to kill. Except for two – one involved a bikie member who Keres had cut off while driving and the other involved the retired fighter, Steve. Steve didn't have much fight motive to kill Keres but definitely had personal motive and ability to kill from his personal loss. The officer also noticed that there was no known toxin detected, as it was written in every report. That wording suggested to the junior officer that there might have been a toxin they missed.

The junior officer quickly ran to his boss' desk and shared his theory. Upon a quick search by the boss, the bikie member was in gaol the week of Keres' murder, which left Steve as their prime suspect. Steve had the motive as Keres' driving led to Steve's family dying, and Steve was a fighter who had the ability. Now they just had to prove it.

Steve was now the prime suspect. There was not enough evidence to charge Steve yet, but some officers believed that something would show up. Jerry believed it was worth chatting to Steve again to see if Steve said anything incriminating or otherwise helpful to the investigation.

Jerry was further encouraged to continue searching for a suspect by several of his higher ups. Keres was connected, he was showy, he was apparently charismatic. This meant that several senior officers were unofficially good friends with Keres. When Keres was killed, they wanted answers and used or abused their power in the hope of getting them.

From the outside the investigation into Keres' death appeared to have stalled.

However, within the station Jerry and several other officers were motivated to have an outcome. Motivated to solve a perplexing crime, and motivated to keep their jobs.

Jerry and Steve

Since officially retiring from fighting, Steve had gone into a simple routine. It wasn't the severe depression routine he had previously, but it was basic. He attempted to leave the house at least once a week to do his shopping in person instead of ordering to his door. He chose a quiet store that no one he knew shopped at, to reduce having to answer the same questions about his fight career and fight end. One day Steve visited the shop and ran into Jerry.

Steve was very surprised to see Jerry in the area as he hadn't thought about meeting anyone he knew. Jerry pretended he hadn't been surveying Steve and acted surprised to see him at the shops, and the two began talking. They then discussed how life had changed for Steve over the last several years with the loss of his family, then his fight career and then finally his fighting retirement. They discussed how Jerry had been promoted to the rank of Inspector and that the tools Steve had taught Jerry a lifetime ago had helped with his personal and professional life.

The promotion meant more money for his family but also meant more stress. Steve and Jerry shared some more random bits of information and some small talk. Jerry asked Steve what he was doing now and Steve replied, "still figuring that one out", and Steve's posture then changed suggesting he was about to continue shopping.

Jerry's tone of voice quickly changed. Steve noticed this but pretended not to notice. Jerry then spoke with Steve and said "I don't know if you know anything about what happened with Keres, but you are currently a prime suspect. I am only telling you this as you once helped me when I was in a bind, so if you do know anything about what happened, it might be best for you to visit the station".

Jerry continued divulging too much information. He then shared with Steve that "some of the junior officers are putting pieces together. Each time they find more pieces, the jigsaw puzzle is looking more like you Steve. So please, if you know anything, please tell me now".

Steve thanked Jerry for the tip knowing that Jerry again, should not be sharing such information. Steve assured Jerry he only knew what the news had reported and then walked away.

Jerry was unconvinced but also realised he had again overshared information with Steve, possibly hoping that it would be enough to make Steve confess through his remorse. However, Jerry also knew he just needed his junior officer to continue building the case and if there was enough evidence that pointed to Steve, then Jerry would be the one to arrest him. Jerry had a lot of faith his in junior officer's ability, and that faith was enough to help Jerry calm himself and refocus, at least for now.

Steve was calm the entire conversation with Jerry, at least on the outside. Inside, he was nervous, he didn't exactly wear a balaclava the night of Keres' murder. He was too impressed with himself that night with his paralytic he had developed. He also knew his rage fuelled push kick meant that he might have been sloppy enough for a clever person to build a case, although they would have to be very clever indeed not to mention very lucky.

Steve finished his shopping and then drove home. While Steve was driving home after the conversation with Jerry, he thought about how well he did at killing Keres. Despite his rage fuelled kick and the lack of balaclava, could they pin this on Steve? Afterall, the police had already asked witnesses, and no one reportedly saw anything. Steve felt he was at a *sliding doors moment*. Should he honour his deceased family and study medicine (something that he had thought about for many years but hadn't because of the cost of studying and because he didn't like touching other people), or should he honour his darker side and remove people who were cancerous for society?

It was a lot to think about.

Sliding Doors?

There are moments in life that everyone experiences, whether they are conscious of these or not. These moments are often small initially but change the direction of a person's life in drastic ways later.

Steve sat on his conundrum for several weeks. It had the potential to be a sliding doors moment that would change him forever. He initially felt that he must choose one of the two options. Studying medicine would allow him to help people and perhaps even save lives of people injured in car accidents, whereas embracing his darker side had the potential to save lives in a different way and involved working outside the law.

After much thought, Steve finally decided to study medicine at the local university. He used his knowledge from his job in health to help him prepare the application. He had sat on the interview panel many years earlier as a community member where he had been partly responsible for which students were successful in the second stage of the interviews, so he knew how to prepare.

He applied for the medical degree and after the three-stage interview process was successful. His preparation had paid off. His wife used to say that he underprepared for these types of things so if she were alive, Steve felt she would have been proud. The following year he began his new life as a medical student. Steve kept to himself as much as possible, only interacting when forced to by the curriculum or other university tasks. He wasn't interested in making friends, at least not now.

The first year flew by, in a "blink and you miss it" kind of way. He learned some new health related information, but most of it was still relatively easy and similar to what he had already learned. Towards the end of the first year the students were told that they would be doing placements. They were advised that the university would be finding their placements on a tier system, but if they could organise approved placements themselves, they should be able to get their first choice.

Also during the first year of study, a lady had approached Steve offering him *contractor* work, work he had kind of done before. Work that was relevant to his previous sliding door conundrum. After much thought Steve eventually accepted the *contractor* work while studying.

At the beginning of his second year, Steve began contacting his old health networks to help organise placements. The university was supportive of this as most of their administrative job was being done for them. The second year flew by also. Steve learned a lot and used some of this knowledge for his *contractor* work.

By the end of the third year, he has passed all his university assessments and placements. He has also continued working his side job as a *contractor* and he felt he was establishing a work life balance. He no longer had to worry about the sliding doors conundrum.

Keres Investigation Deepens

Several years had passed since Keres was murdered. The junior officer was eventually promoted and passed the case onto the next junior officer. Because of the money and social status of Keres prior to his death, there were still some powerful people calling for the investigation to find the murderer. There were still powerful people putting pressure on Jerry and the station to find an answer, and to find the perpetrator.

The Keres case still had many unanswered questions. If it had of happened to a normal person, no one would have cared, and it would be left as "an unsolved robbery gone wrong". But Keres was not a normal person, so these questions needed answers. Questions like how did a professional fighter in his prime get murdered by his car door and have no defensive wounds? How would an athlete known for speed and power be stationary long enough for that to happen with no signs he tried to fight back? The new junior officer also rediscovered a previously forgotten question, a question that some of the original officers had asked before they had then dismissed it. Why was the white blood cell count so high when Keres was so drunk?

The new junior officer O'Sullivan took over the case and revisited all the evidence. Officer O'Sullivan grew up with two parents who were research doctors and learnt a lot about health from a young age, more than most of their peers. O'Sullivan's father specialised in diseases and their mother specialised in the nervous system. O'Sullivan was not overly interested in what their parents did growing up and always had the urge to be a police officer.

While O'Sullivan was revisiting the evidence to date, they noted something odd. They noticed that Keres had an abnormally high level of white blood cells. This wasn't spectacular information but something about this flagged O'Sullivan's interest. That weekend O'Sullivan visited their parents and began talking about an interesting case, making sure to deidentify the information.

O'Sullivan visited their parents for dinner. Towards the end of the night, they told their parents they wanted to discuss an odd finding in a case. Their parents were intrigued as O'Sullivan rarely spoke work with them. O'Sullivan asked them about white blood cells. O'Sullivan asked if an abnormally high count of white blood cells would suggest a health condition or odd poison response. Both parents were somewhat proud that their child had actually listened as a child, although they didn't let this show.

They both confirmed from their very differing fields of medical research that yes, high white blood cell counts are important to follow up on but can't determine poison or disease on its own. O'Sullivan then asked if alcohol can cause white blood cells to increase. The parents share that whilst it is possible, normally alcohol caused the cell count to decrease, not increase.

After O'Sullivan finished the dinner with their parents, they chose to go back to the station instead of going home. They called Jerry asking for overtime approval and clearance approval to continue the investigation as they had some leads they wanted to follow. After a very brief lecture about work life balance, Jerry gave O'Sullivan the required approvals needed.

Using the government health data base, they had access to at work, and after making few calls and taking a heap of notes, O'Sullivan read through Keres' medical records again. O'Sullivan found that Keres had no white blood count abnormalities recorded historically. O'Sullivan completed further research, and the following day confirmed with their parents again, that if a person had no white blood cell abnormality history and was heavily intoxicated, then if anything the person should have had a lower-than-average white blood cell count.

O'Sullivan was now confident that whoever murdered Keres with his car door, used some form of natural poison to weaken or paralyse him first. O'Sullivan shared this with his boss Jerry as an update, although there was still no evidence that it was Steve.

Jerry was intrigued by everything O'Sullivan has just told him. He thanked O'Sullivan and suggested they keep up the good work to see if they find anything else that could help.

A gut instinct or a paranoia kept directing Jerry to Steve, but no one was arrested because of a gut instinct. Steve had motive, had physical ability but did not at least on paper, posses the knowledge to poison someone without any toxicological evidence.

Again, there was not enough evidence to charge Steve. Especially since he too had access to good lawyers, and again on paper at least, was an upstanding member of society with just enough fame to make a wrongful arrest cause further stress to Jerry and the station.

With this new information and interpretations from O'Sullivan and their parents, Jerry had an urge to revisit other unsolved cases. He wasn't sure why he had this urge but was willing to try anything to have the Keres case solved.

These other cases were similar to the Keres' one from the medical perspective. They were all relatively healthy, had no obvious signs of injury, and some had higher than normal white blood cell counts. However, since the victims were not famous, there wasn't much follow up until now. These cases had all occurred in the last three years, and they all included families that were sure their loved one was murdered. They all included evidence that suggested that the deceased people had died by natural causes.

Was this bigger than just a personal vendetta against Keres?

Steve's Contracting

One of Keres' estranged lovers was at the bar the night Keres was killed. They didn't see Keres be murdered, but they did see Steve grab something from Keres' chest area and then walk away. They didn't say anything to the police because part of them was glad that someone had finally killed Keres.

The estranged lover had been beaten several times during their relationship with Keres, but no one ever believed them, and Keres' lawyers made sure the estranged lover never told anyone publicly.

One afternoon, after Steve had almost finished his first year of study he received a letter. The letter said if Steve was willing, that they would like to meet, and in the bottom of the letter was two smudged words with one word looking like Keres. This was unsettling for Steve as he had thought that the police had no leads and he was therefore in the clear.

The meeting place was in a public location, near where Steve normally shopped, so he decided to go there to see what it was about. He decided that if the stranger was too aggressive or accused him publicly, he would just leave.

Once Steve arrived at the location, he sat there and waited. Several people walked past and Steve kept anticipating that anyone of these people must be the stranger. Steve was starting to become restless and decided he would wait a few more minutes before leaving. Just as he was about to leave, an older attractive lady walked towards him.

Steve wasn't blind, he knew what he looked like. He was still relatively fit but felt that he wasn't the most attractive man, nor was famous enough anymore. He felt that this lady was too attractive to be wanting to flirt with Steve, so he paid extra attention in case this was the stranger.

As expected, the lady approached him. She introduced herself as a fan of Steve and thanked him for his previous entertaining fights. The message of what she said was normal enough, but it was her exact word choice that was odd. The lady said "she was a fan of Steve" specifically and then thanked him for the fights. It felt odd, it felt like she had emphasised *fan* a little too much. Maybe he was just thinking too much about it, so he tried to push this concern down. Steve thanked her for the kindness and was about to walk away when The Fan mentioned the letter.

The Fan sat down and Steve obliged. The Fan mentioned that they wanted Steve to listen to everything they had to say before responding or leaving. Steve reluctantly agreed in case this was something to do with Keres as the smudged word had suggested.

The Fan talked about Keres almost as soon as Steve had sat down. She explained that Keres was not a nice person behind closed doors and that at one point they had been lovers. The Fan also explained that she had applied for several Domestic Violence Orders, only for Keres' lawyers to eventually encourage her to sign the Non-Disclosure Agreement. She needed the money, so she accepted.

She then explained to Steve that she was at the bar the night Keres had died. She went on to say also that she saw someone who looked almost exactly like Steve grab something off Keres' chest area and then walk away. She then explained that she wasn't interested in money or to telling the police, but she knew of several other women in DV situations that could benefit from whatever Steve had used to immobilise Keres.

The Fan then explained that since signing the NDA she had enough money to live a well-off life and therefore had enough to pay Steve for his services. If Steve agreed, all he had to do is return to the same location tomorrow and they would then discuss the next steps. She promised to pay Steve well and that he would be doing the world a favour.

Until this point Steve had been silent. He had maintained a calm exterior but was very nervous internally. He thanked The Fan for her conversation and then returned home. That night Steve couldn't sleep. Part of him wanted to activate his darkness again, but the other part wanted to study medicine.

To distract himself, Steve put on a streaming service and watched the 'Lethal Weapon' movies. He hoped that watching these old police movies he had seen many times before, would be enough to distract him, so that in the morning he would return to focusing on his studies. Eventually at around two am Steve fell asleep with the movies playing in the background.

Steve had grown up in with violence. He had witnessed physical domestic violence and for obvious reasons, he didn't like the idea of smaller people being attacked without recompense or justice. He decided to meet The Fan one more time to find out the details including payment. He didn't need the money at the moment but was aware his wife's life insurance would run out eventually and he didn't want to risk losing the home he had built with his late wife Stephanie.

Steve met The Fan at the agreed upon location and time and Steve was informed that The Fan would hire him officially as a senior Janitor and Groundkeeper

Contractor so that any money will be above board for the taxation office. The money would be enough to pay for any expenses and cover the cost of an average mortgage in a year.

Steve agreed and decided he would visit The Fan at her residence the next Saturday. He was nervous all week, but a part of him was also relieved. Instead of a sliding moment where he had to choose, he might be able to live in both worlds at once. One world involved studying medicine and being a good person helping people and saving lives.

The other world where he killed society's rot which also meant he would be indirectly saving lives. With Stephanie gone, Steve no longer had the social moral compass that would have highlighted how outrageous his thinking had become. To Steve, he was being logical and making the world a better place, for the greater good.

Steve arrived at the residence given to him by The Fan. Once there he felt uneasy. He initially assumed that it was to do with his new contracting role, but something about The Fan felt off. Something about The Fan also seemed oddly familiar. Steve tried to ignore this, eventually successfully, although he would later find out why The Fan felt so odd and familiar. The Fan then gave Steve the context and the details of his contracting work.

She explained that when she became a victim of DV it made her want to help other victims. She wasn't sure how she wanted to help until she saw someone walk away from Keres' dead body. Seeing Steve walk away gave The Fan hope and direction and gave her clarity about how to help and what to spend her NDA money on.

The Fan provided Steve his first target. She provided him with the context of the DV victim, how the police hadn't been able to help stop the alleged perpetrator or help the victim. The Fan answered any questions Steve had, trying her best to reassure Steve. Steve agreed to work for her as a contractor, as long as it didn't impact on his study time.

Steve then returned home and revisited his dart gun and darts. He hadn't used these in a long time and had to reacquaint himself with them. He reviewed his concoction and tweaked it with what he had learned in his recent study. He ensured there was no trace of his DNA anywhere on the dart by practicing the same health and safety practice doctors and hospitals preached. Over the next two years Steve studied medicine during the week, spending many hours at the library. Occasionally he would receive a coded text from The Fan and would visit her to receive the context, information and target.

Steve believed he was doing good work by clearing targets from The Fan's list. The Fan was very believable, and it made Steve feel important in a way he didn't yet understand. What Steve didn't know was that whilst The Fan's targets were men who all had DVOs against them that were squashed by the law; they were also men who The Fan believed had wronged her, either directly or indirectly, throughout her life. Steve wasn't saving victims; he had become The Fan's personal assassin for hire.

When he wasn't studying or contracting, he spent his time at home staring at the photos of his deceased family. He had kept these photos clean but hadn't been able to remove them off the wall. A part of Steve still felt that by leaving them on the wall, they were still with him, and he was not alone. He didn't cry much when he looked at them anymore, rather it helped him to feel grounded. It also gave him motivation to study and to complete contracts when his internal motivation for either was waning. This suggested there was still a bit of his mongrel in the background, festering.

Jerry and O'Sullivan

Jerry reviewed some unsolved cases that had similar patterns to the Keres file. He found that there were several victims in the town who all had oddly high levels of white blood cells. Jerry had found several other victims dating back eight years but felt these were not connected as his gut (or his paranoia) told him that it was Steve. As a result of his gut, Jerry ruled the other cases out. After the conversation with O'Sullivan the week prior, Jerry felt that some of the unsolved cases and the Keres case must be linked.

Jerry still had his suspicions about Steve, but without evidence, his suspicions were starting to feel like paranoia. He returned to O'Sullivan and asked them to investigate those extra cases to ensure that their medical records had all been clear prior to the death. Jerry didn't need to explain but felt it would help motivate

O'Sullivan. Jerry explained to O'Sullivan that he had a theory that their prime suspect in the Keres case might be linked to these other unsolved cases.

O'Sullivan spends the next few days making calls and researching files and finds that of the files Jerry provided, there were four people who had no prior medical issues and that all died on a Saturday from apparent natural causes. O'Sullivan then shared these findings with Jerry. Again, it was slim, but slim was better than nothing. Especially if Jerry was correct, Steve has gone from a murderer to a serial killer.

Together Jerry and O'Sullivan established that the four victims all shared only one thing in common with each other and with Keres. They had all had DVOs put against them only for the DVOs to be squashed by the courts. Again, it was a weak connection, but any correlation had a chance to be useful. With enough weak correlations you get connections, and with enough connections, you have a case.

It was nearing the end of the year, and it had been much more stressful than Jerry originally anticipated. He knew his promotion would mean more stress, but the Keres situation and the subsequent pressure from senior ranks and other powerful people, and the possibility of a serial killer in his town, all meant that Jerry had been working too much. In an odd twist, Steve had taught Jerry tools to help with relationship stress which had been helping Jerry, but now Steve was the cause of his long working hours and as a result, meant that Jerry had to practice these tools more to save his marriage.

It was a Friday afternoon, and Jerry received a phone call from the local coroner that Jerry had called earlier that week. The coroner reported that they had a body who appears to have died from natural causes with the only suspicious thing about the death being the very high white blood cell count. Due to Jerry's call earlier in the week, the coroner had been remaining extra alert for such abnormalities. The family also insisted the person was healthy and insisted that their family member could not have died by natural causes and they wanted the police to treat this as a murder investigation.

The next working day Jerry and O'Sullivan find that this victim also had DVOs squashed by the court. Jerry asked his bosses if he could use two civilian medical researchers to help solve Keres' cold case. After explaining how these experts could assist, the senior ranks agreed and Jerry invited O'Sullivan's parents onto the case. Given their uniquely useful medical research backgrounds, it was hoped that they would provide another weak link that could break the case wide open. Or at least that was Jerry's hope.

Jerry and O'Sullivan explained the situation to O'Sullivan's parents. They explained the importance of the Keres cold case and the five new victims. Jerry, officer O'Sullivan and O'Sullivan's two parents spent the next two months researching and following leads.

To The Fore/Fourth

Steve was attending his fourth year of medical school. He hoped his study and placements would go well and he was fully focused. He now owned his house completely and had been earning enough money that study was now a want and not a need, as he had no financial stress.

It was week four and already Steve felt like he had read four months' worth of information. His Saturday contractor job had been relatively easy as work was only twice to three times a year and his formula used in his dart gun had continued to improve, especially with some of the information he learned in his last placement at the hospital, and the chemicals he was able to "borrow".

Unknown to Steve, by making his paralytic more lethal, it also meant it was easier to trace. His initial concoctions had been to close to nature, but with the addition of the hospital chemical, the unnecessary increase in lethality meant it was now different enough that in the unlikely event that someone was still investigating him, they might be able to trace the chemical. The last several years of study meant Steve had been embracing his intelligence. The last several years of successful paralytic kills meant that unknown to him, his ego had increased while his wisdom and carefulness had decreased.

Over the last several months the O'Sullivan's and Jerry had been hard at work. They had realised that whatever concoction was being used, that it had become more potent and more lethal based on the now ridiculous levels of white blood cells. Why would someone who had previously killed people with a paralytic change their poison? Upon, further analysis of the latest victim, it looked like an ingredient had been used that could be traceable. This was the lucky break Jerry was hoping for. After a few tests by the O'Sullivan parents and Jerry and officer O'Sullivan following up on some leads, they found two locations in the area that used this chemical. One at the local hospital and one at the local nail parlour.

Jerry asked O'Sullivan to check the nail parlour while he checked the hospital. Jerry's investigation was fruitful with his paranoia appearing to be gut instinct. After speaking with several of the hospital clinical nurses, Jerry was informed that Steve had completed a placement at the hospital around the same time the O'Sullivan medical researchers suggested the concoction improved. The nurses also confirmed that the hospital used this chemical when treating certain diseases.

Somewhat sad for Steve, but excited that he wasn't "crazy", Jerry travelled back to the station. Once there he was about to share the news with O'Sullivan, but O'Sullivan also appeared to have found something. Jerry asked O'Sullivan for their update. O'Sullivan explained to Jerry that a wealthy lady had recently begun purchasing a special chemical that the nail parlour used in their artwork made from organic materials. They said that the chemical was very expensive and came with a warning that if ingested it could cause death.

The nail parlour said they didn't advertise this and didn't normally sell it, but this lady was insistent and offered them a lot more money than what it was worth, so they accepted. They didn't know her full name, but she always signed with a picture of a Sensu, a Geisha fan, instead of her name. O'Sullivan felt there was a connection between the case and this lady but was unsure what exactly.

Jerry then shared his news with O'Sullivan. He shared that Steve had completed a placement at the hospital at the same time as the breakthrough, so now they had two potential suspects. Steve was still the primary suspect, but maybe this Sensu or fan lady was an accomplice.

Four more months pass, and Steve is doing well at university and decided that he no longer wanted to work for The Fan as a contractor any longer. He had his fill of murdering people, no matter how evil they might have been, and wanted to fully focus on medicine. He arrived at The Fan's residence unexpectedly and attempted to explain to her his decision. As Steve had feared, The Fan did not take the news well and threatened to expose Steve to the police. This angered Steve.

He threatened to go to the police about her so they would both go down together. The Fan then oddly changed her tone and body language, a little too quickly for Steve to feel comfortable. She then apologised for overreacting and offered to pour Steve a drink from the kitchen. Steve initially declined given what he knew of poisons but eventually he was persuaded by The Fan and agreed. With Steve's increase in ego and reduction in wisdom, the thought that The Fan would try and poison him, oddly didn't cross his mind.

Steve waited by the couch while The Fan was pouring the drinks. Just as The Fan had almost finished pouring the drinks, with a special drink for Steve and a normal drink for herself, there was a knock at the door. The knocking at the door spooked The Fan and she accidently spilled some of the special mixture meant for Steve's drink.

She noticed some on the floor and quickly cleaned it up but didn't notice where else it spilled. Steve volunteered to check the knock at the door, collected the postal order and brought it into the kitchen area for The Fan. Steve sees the name on the parcel as Francine but doesn't think anything of it considering the only Francine he knew was when he was a young child.

The Fan then thanked Steve and while she was putting the package away Steve grabbed what he thought was his glass and moved the other glass to the right to dry up some spillage with his shirt. He then sat down and consumed the drink quickly so that he could then leave. The Fan then grabbed what she thought was her drink and then sat next to Steve and also consumed her drink quickly.

Once The Fan was finished drinking, her body language changes quickly again. She laughed at Steve. Her laughter was odd, it resembled a cartoon villain's laugh a little too much. Through her laughter she then said to Steve "you don't remember me do you". Steve was very confused by this. The Fan saw his confusion on his face and said, "I don't mean working for me, I mean you don't remember me from when you were younger do you"? Steve was still confused and felt that The Fan had become even more unstable. She then shared that she had attended the same school as Steve when they were younger. Steve was several grades younger and was an easy target. Steve had reminded her of a person she didn't like at home so she would tease him. Then one day he had for no reason, as far as she could tell, dthrown her into the metal drinking troughs and then walked away.

Steve then remembers the name on the parcel and the school yard incident. Steve remained still and very confused about how these worlds had come together. He then slowly has a sudden realisation about why he had felt so uneasy with The Fan this whole time.

Steve responded explaining that he had completely forgotten about the school event as they were both children. He shared that he had indeed thrown her into that trough as a child as he had anger issues and because she had been targeting him. He explained that he only threw her as self-defence as she had on that day decided to swing at him. Steve explained that he had only been defending himself against a much larger and aggressive target.

He then highlights that the event was a very long time ago and that they were both just kids. Francine confirmed part of Steve's recollection of events. They were both kids and she did tease him, but she strongly believed, no she knew that she never swung at Steve and that his response unfairly escalated the situation. Francine also shared that the moment her face hit the trough she decided she would have her revenge on "people like Steve".

Steve was now feeling slightly unwell and wanted to flee the residence, but his legs were feeling heavy. He looked at The Fan

Francine and she laughed again. As she was laughing, she said that she had poisoned him. She highlighted the irony that a person who had killed people with poison would then die by poison. Unknown to Steve his drink had received a splash of the poison from Francine when she got spooked by the post at her door.

Steve thought that this was odd behaviour as throughout their dealings, The Fan had always acted as if she was submissive, almost lacking confidence. But this sudden information and body language changes shocked Steve almost as much as finding out he had been poisoned. Steve then feels odd and feints. Francine is the last thing he sees as he blinks to unconsciousness.

Jerry and O'Sullivan had decided that they would go and get both suspects. After many years of "gut feelings" and weak connections Jerry had had several quick breakthroughs. First the tracing of the chemical thanks to officer O'Sullivan's parents, and then the DNA on the signed piece of paper at the nail salon. Whilst the paper had no name or address, by signing the Sensu image, she had left DNA evidence. The DNA evidence allowed them to find the residence of a person called Francine Annabel Nicolls.

Since it would be O'Sullivan's first house arrest Jerry offered to go with O'Sullivan. They decided to arrest Francine for purchasing the chemical from the nail parlour first under suspicion of murder, then they would arrest Steve, with Jerry taking the lead.

O'Sullivan knocked on the door, and no one answered. O'Sullivan then knocked again, and there was still no answer. Jerry looked through the glass window to see two people on the floor not moving. Jerry gives O'Sullivan permission to open the door by force. They entered the residence and found something unexpected. Jerry cleared the area while O'Sullivan checked for a pulse. He found a slight pulse on the male, but no pulse on the female.

Jerry confirmed this while the paramedics were called. Jerry confirmed that the male was Steve and the female was Francine who had been buying the chemical from the nail parlour. Steve was taken to the hospital unconscious, and Francine was declared dead on site and taken to the coroner's office. Over the next week junior officers were assigned to Steve's bed in case he woke while Jerry completed the paperwork. No next of kin could be found for Francine and the file was almost ready to be closed.

Just as Jerry felt he had finished with Francine's file he received a call from the federal police. When a photo of Francine was leaked to the press in suspicion of

Keres' murder the federal police became interested.

Their team thought that Francine looked a lot like one of their persons of interest. After they gained access to her DNA, they confirmed that she was the person of interest known by the code name Faded Amber Nightshade or FAN for short. Her code name was given because she specialised in disguising herself behind soft, unthreatening personas, her faded amber hair colour, gentle mannerisms, and muted presence, yet struck with precision in the darkness, leaving no trace. She was the perfect nightshade: beautiful, overlooked, and lethal.

The federal police then take over the investigation, despite Jerry's complaints and protests. They shared with Jerry and his superiors that the FAN or Francine as Jerry had called her, had been killing males for at least the last eight years that they knew of. They determined that Steve was merely the next victim of the FAN and any wrongdoing that Jerry's and O'Sullivan's reports suggested were to be thrown out as they didn't fit their extensive research and decision.

The federal police officially charge the now deceased FAN with the murder of Keres and at least thirteen other known victims. The junior police officers were then withdrawn from Steve's bedside.

But there are still so many unanswered questions for Jerry and O'Sullivan. If this Francine lady was really the FAN as the federal police say, why did she need Steve at all? Why was Steve really at Francine's residence if he had no DVO history? Why after pulling Francine's and Steve's bank records was she paying Steve as a janitor and paying him more than most doctors are paid? Why did Steve accept this work when he was studying at medical school and had enough money without contracting work?

Jerry had to stop O'Sullivan. O'Sullivan was making very valid points with the questions but unfortunately, they had to work within the constraints of the law and that meant sometimes questions remained unanswered. It meant that sometimes jurisdictions and ranks influence a case more than the evidence. Sometimes it meant that despite what an officer might feel is the truth, the official evidence is all that matters.

O'Sullivan was not happy with this and began to protest so Jerry sent O'Sullivan home. O'Sullivan was unhappy enough that they thought they thought they might even leave the police service altogether. If bureaucratic practices were more important than the truth than what was the point in being a police officer. There might be other ways that they could help to stop criminals. Other ways that didn't have to work with the red tape and bureaucracy that existed. They would sleep on these thoughts for now.

Steve woke in hospital unsure what had happened. The last thing he remembered was being told by The Fan or Francine, that he was poisoned, he remembered trying to move, not being able to and then feinting. Slightly afraid still, he calls for a nurse by pressing the buzzer beside his pillow. A lady enters the room and asks if Steve is okay. Steve was still not fully awake as he had been asleep for at least a week, but he felt a sudden sense of dread. He ignored this, assuming it was his mind playing tricks and answered the question.

Steve replied that he thought he was okay but wanted to know if the *nurse* knew what happened to the lady that was with him. The *Nurse* replied she didn't know anything about that, but she was sure that the head nurse would be able to help

Steve. The *Nurse* then tells Steve that there were officers by his bed until yesterday and that this must mean that whatever they thought Steve did must have been incorrect.

She then began to walk closer to Steve's head. She checked the room and leant in. She then whispered, "I can't help you with any questions about a lady, but what I want you to know is that I had always been you're your biggest Fan". The *Nurse* quickly and quietly leaves the room. She walked past a nurse on the way to Steve's room and then exited the building.

The nurse on duty in Steve's area entered the room to find Steve asleep. She felt this was odd considering Steve's button had only recently been pressed requesting assistance. The nurse was slightly annoyed at what she believed to be malfunctioning equipment. As she was about to leave the room, she noticed on the TV a photo was being shown on the news. She stopped and paid attention to the news story as something caught her eye.

The news story discusses that the federal police had issued an official statement. They stated that a lady known as Francine was responsible for killing Keres and at least thirteen other people. However, unfortunately this lady was now deceased. Families could now rest easier knowing they at least have closure.

The nurse was confused. The lady she just saw leaving Steve's area, was an almost identical match to the photo on the news. Part of her wanted to call her clinical nurse manager and discuss this, but she assumed she was mistaken and instead talked herself out of it. She assumed she was mistaken and then continued with her work and went to the next patient.

After the federal police's official story was released and everyone at the station celebrated Jerry and O'Sullivan's hard work, Jerry sat at his desk. Relieved that the case was officially closed, but unhappy that there were still too many unanswered questions. Just then he received a call from the coroner. The coroner told Jerry that "the lady on his table in front of him who is supposed to be Francine, does not match the DNA of the actual Francine".

This was odd as until now the DNA had been a match. Could FAN have influenced the testing? This new information suggested something else, possibly more nefarious was at work. Jerry thanked the coroner for the update. He hung up the phone up. Closed his door. Then screamed in frustration.

www.ingramcontent.com/pod-product-compliance
Lightning Source LLC
Chambersburg PA
CBHW070458170726
48291CB00008B/2563